The Damsel Fly
and other stories

by

Barbara Kremen

Ravenna Press, 2006

The illustrations are reproduced from original collages by Irwin
Kremen, and are independent of the text.

Settignano IV 1969-70 (cover)
de novo 1993-94 (The Damsel Fly)
*Lungarno 1977 (*Ponte Vecchio*)*
Make Fast 1980 (Deceit of Snow)

Also by Barbara Kremen:
Out Of (poetry)
Tree Trove (fiction)

FIRST EDITION

Published by Ravenna Press
PO Box 127, Edmonds, WA 98020 US
www.ravennapress.com
Printed in the United States

For Krem, always

The Damsel Fly

Prologue

"I will not have a D & C," she said.

"I will keep the baby," she said.

"I will not marry him. I want nothing to do with him at all."

Ellen spoke with the patient reasonableness of a clerk refusing something to a client of low intelligence. Her mother, after a week of it, was still not used to this cold hostility.

"I guess I've said all I can," Paula said nevertheless.

Ellen looked at her mother with suddenly furious blue eyes.

"*I* had no father."

"That was different. I was in my fifth month. His family had the marriage annulled. I didn't qualify."

Paula smoothed her damp gloves carefully in her lap, and crumpled them again into a ball. It's Henry, she thought.

She stood up. She had never removed her coat; the gas burner in Ellen's bleak little room couldn't cope with the clammy chill of a London November.

"My plane leaves tomorrow, early. I'm going back to the hotel. You can call me if you want, or, you know, if you should want to change your mind."

Her daughter stood up too, taller than her mother by a half a foot. "Goodbye mother," she said and closed the door.

Paula held her fur piece tightly to her throat with one hand and steadied herself on the banister with the other. She crept carefully down the three flights; her ears were ringing and a dull pain throbbed at the base of her skull. She dismissed the thought of going back and asking Ellen to help her get a cab. She was a tiny woman with birdlike bones, the carriage of a martinet and the face of an extraordinarily wrinkled doll.

A faint smell of roses was all that materially remained of Paula's visit with its arguments, pleas, promises, forebodings. Another objection, that of miscegenation, hung sourly over their heads but was never broached. Paula hadn't dared.

Ellen flung up her window and looked down at the dark little rear court. The dank draft blotted out the lingering scent of Paula's rosewater. Ellen shivered. She was already late for work. She hurried down the stairs. On the way she passed, and would scarcely have noticed if the blocked noon traffic hadn't been so unusually strident, a wrecker being chained to a cab that had ploughed into a police box.

A few blocks from Ellen's room her mother lay sprawled on the pavement. The door of the cab hung on one hinge and the crumpled hood was wedged against a police box. When the ambulance arrived the crowd that coagulates within seconds at the site of an accident drew back in silence. A passer-by picked up Paula's purse and stepped up to the still figure being strapped to a stretcher. Blood ran onto the glass-eyed fox head nestling on her collarbone. He laid the purse on her stomach as they hoisted her into the ambulance.

It took the hospital hours to reach the husband on the other side of the Atlantic for permission to operate. By the time they cut the tumor from Paula's brain she was dead, though this delay would probably have made no difference in her case.

Three thousand miles away the voice, traveling at the speed of sound, summoned Henry from sleep. With it everything changed. Yet everything remained the same. He dressed, put water on to boil, drank coffee, packed a bag, and made a number of phone calls. Voices flew back and forth across the ocean. Finally it was Ellen's voice and he was telling her what had happened a few blocks from her door. Then Henry too was flying over the ocean. He met Ellen at the hospital. He made arrangements. They sat and talked.

Ellen was grudging with words, gave him the barest account, volunteered nothing.

Several days later he flew again across the Atlantic, this time carrying a small cardboard box.

The Watchers

The excited air of noon shimmers in the heat and whirr of wings, so swift, so clear, as to be almost invisible, until turning they catch the sun's dazzle. Long jeweled bodies, sapphire, topaz, lapis, flash above the wrinkled water and their fractured images stain the pond with bent bars of color.

Coursers, harriers, hoverers, perchers, they divvy up the levels of the sky. The largest and swiftest, streaks of bright blue, gaudy green, sweep tirelessly back and forth on high "in long sinuous curves;" at mid-level swirls a troupe with pale blue bodies, turquoise heads and gold tinctured wings. At the margins of the pond flutters one smaller yet, wings flavescent, body ruby-red, jet striped, face "with the whiteness and subopaqueness of fine china."

It is an aerial dance, a medley, a chase. They veer in dizzying circles, spiral, glide, dodge, soar, recede. They stop short in mid-air, hover with blurred trilling wings, dart and hover and dart again. Loop-the-loops, hairpin turns, kamikaze dives, backward rolls; these are the acrobats of the sky. They have split-second control; not one comes tumbling from the air.

Now comes a pair in chase, white with brown-brindled wings. One harries the other skyward. As though swept in an updraught they lift and fall, the pursuer flying up and over and around his quarry until they disappear from view.   Closer to shore a bronzy-green wheel slowly passes over the water, two arched bodies in a linked embrace, lovers light upon the wind.

A stranger leaps to center, long, elegant, blue-black from head to forked tail, and the troupe scatters wheeling around him. He soars, pauses with a whirring entrechat of wings, exits into the trees.

One now comes to rest on a bending reed. He holds his four great gauzy wings outspread that seemed in flight of merely denser air; they sparkle in quicksilver scales.   Through the taut translucent membrane, one ten-thousandth of a millimeter thick, the sun throws into relief an intricate mesh of veins. Two close-set ribs, as though drawn by a fine black pen, brace the wing's upper edge, then meet at the curve, the point of greatest pressure from the air, in a tawny rectangle of horn.   Six other strong ribs branch downward; between them a crisscross of thread-like veins forms that rich pattern of quadrangles and hexagons, according to spaces narrow, spaces wide, so incidentally pleasing to the eye.

These venations are as thumbprints to the species. The size and color of that smudged chitinous patch that joins the upper costal and radial veins, the presence or absence of the bisector of the anal loop, the angles, curved or abrupt, of the trigonal planate, these and other small specificities will distinguish Aeshna from Gynacantha, Sympetrum from the Libellula. The big green and blue dragonfly now perching on the reed is an Anax, one of the Aeshnidae.

As Agamemnon of the Atridae or Pfaff, the last of the Pfaffnidae.

For Pfaff is watching, and has been since the sun-warmed air of morning called them forth from the woodland. He watches, hunkered on a bank, pad on knee, pencil stuck in a tussock, a patient perspiring man, plagued by mosquitoes, beclouded by gnats. A dark hulk whose head and eyes wag back and forth in measure with that restless choreography.

The Anax perches on the reed, childhood's darning needle that could sew a liar's lips. He perches motionless, a coiled spring at the ready, until his like, meandering past, triggers him. Up he zooms, straight up like a helicopter, and back and forth the reaches of the pond they zigzag, wheeling, banking, head to tail, synchronous in motion as though joined by a string.

Still lord of his four-foot domain he returns alone, swiping midges out of the air with his spiny legs and settles on his reed to watch and warm his glassy wings.

Pfaff raises his field glasses to his eyes. He does this slowly so as not to startle the insect who in any case seems oblivious to this lump in the grass. An enlarged face hangs before him, so monstrous it might in earlier times have sent children screaming from the theatre. A ferocious face with bristly mouth hairs, three black ocelli spots that look like eyes but are not, an enormous bulge encircling the head like a black tire. Beneath this juts a shelf-like plateau that partially conceals the murderous mouth parts, the scoops, prongs and blades necessary to carve, slice and masticate meat. Not for nothing are they called the Odonata, the Toothed Ones.

Eyes to see with, jaws and teeth to bite and chew, a nervous system, a digestive tract, an elaborate reproductive apparatus, the basic ground plan, he reflects, even as you and I. But within that plan, such a strange and alien otherness. This alien otherness fascinates him, predicated, as it must be, by definition, on similarities. Even this whiff of anthropomorphism displeases him and he brushes away the thought as a gnat from his nose.

Eyes to see with, more like 50,000 eyes, tiny facets indented into that pneumatic bulge that encircles the head. Each facet, or ommatidium, is in itself a tiny eye, each has its cornea, its cone, and pigmented retinal cell, connected by a nerve fiber to the optical nerve; each reports a minuscule fragment of reflected light entering simultaneously from above, below, to the sides, the front, behind. What can it be to see everything at once?

They watch each other, the Anax and Pfaff. At least the insect appears to be looking at him; its face is turned in his direction. He corrects himself with some annoyance; if the animal had its back turned wouldn't it still "see" him?

What does it see, he wonders, this insect Argus? Thousands of little "him's" hunkered in the grass, beclouded by gnats? Or rather thousands of tiny pieces of himself, a mosaic of a large inert object to which the Anax gives little heed. It would be vastly more interested in that which flickers, in the dancing cloud of tiny gnats. It is thought that the facets are themselves specialized; those on the lower portion of the bulge registering stationary objects below; those on the upper, objects that move, and even at flight speed the dragonfly can detect, orient to, and swoop upon flying objects far tinier and at far greater distances than the human eye would be capable of discerning, even with field glasses.

How does that rudimentary nervous system process with such rapidity all that simultaneity of information: the bird overhead that could eat him if it choose, the water boatman's spidery tracks, the flight and veer and dash of what comes up from behind, rival or prey or mate? Pfaff, sitting within himself, his two eyes facing forward, extended by two black tubes as on a stalk that grab at distance and bring it close, tries to think himself into a creature which experiences the world in the round.

In his student days and something of a philosopher, existence puzzled him. He would sit for hours cross-legged in a corner, eyes unblinking, Adam's apple pulsing, "being" a frog. People began to find something froglike in his appearance, the wide mouth, the flattened nose, the cold widespread green eyes, the pale freckled skin.

He puts down his glasses, reaches for the pad. The Anax flies off. Each to his business. In the lower passages of the air, working close to shore, a slenderer, more needle-like creature flits restlessly, perches and flits and perches again.   It holds its gauzy wings folded together and upraised, and the cobalt body stretches horizontally into the air like a furled flag or an enameled pin. This is the damselfly, more delicate brother to the dragon.

Pfaff's Notebook

Interloper, thief, snoop. Is this what I, Henry Hazlitt, am become in my late middle age? To appropriate not only this man's house but his notebook and then his pond, in short his life?

Beatrice and I met in the coffee shop at the corner of 87th and Madison. A short stocky woman swathed in fringed shawl and voluminous skirt and carrying an enormous reticule, black hair strained back in a bun, an earnest moon face. She had seen the obituary in the newspaper and written to condole and then again to offer the place. She insisted we meet. She had known Paula years ago, had known Ellen as a child; she knew Paula's story. Her tenant had vanished, a man named Pfaff, she doubted he'd be back any time soon. Such sudden exits were not unusual. It would be a help to her with the rent. For me it could be a retreat. It was all so dreadful . . . Paula and she . . . Two hours later, utterly depleted, I escaped with the key.

The raw dank March day of my arrival. A musty smell that a week stoking the wood stove could not dispel, water pump rusted-stuck from a winter's disuse, no phone, he would have no phone. I picture a burly man, somber, humorless. The place furnished sparely, cluttered with debris, a mess of books and papers on shelves and floor, dusty pickings of the woods—pods, twigs, cones, bark, fronds, grasses, leaves, tossed into foil pans from countless frozen dinners or stuck in jelly jars. Some cobwebby paraphernalia in a corner, an insect net, a fishing rod, an aquarium stained slime green, a thermometer, a meat baster. One wall papered with sketches fastened with thumbtacks, edges curling, watercolors, they seemed to be, of flowers.

It looked as though he got up one day, pushed back his chair so violently as to send it sliding into the center of the room, and left, for good. On the table by the window lay his open penknife, the blade blackened with a gummy crud, a wizened apple core, a rind of cheese gnawed by something down to its dark amber leather. A discolored mug crusted with a brownish residue. The dried stalks of some long coarse weed. There were rows of peculiar little slits up the stems as though he had been methodically scoring them with his knife. "*Nature morte*," I said, startled by the sound of my own voice.

Pfaff's notebook, the same in which I am now writing, lay on the table, a thick cahier, opened about midway, the pages weighed down by a magnifying glass. The left page was covered with a small neat script; the right, blank. The true beginning of this record starts there on the left page where he had written:

Aug.10. Tiny slits spaced evenly down the stem, extending below the waterline, about 1/4 inch apart in vertical rows. Inside each slit six eggs, minute milky-white cylinders with pointed reddish tips. The eggs are translucent; a vague shadow of something inside. Two spots at one end that look like eyes. The plant seems to have scarred over. How does the creature get out?

Aug. 13. Something going on inside the eggs, a kind of rhythmic pumping action, a swelling. All this seen under the glass.

Aug.16. Attended a hatching at the pond. First a barely visible tip protruded, gradually lengthening into a tiny thread-like worm. The pointed tip of the egg will have kept the slit from entirely closing over. As it emerged it began to whip back and forth until it finally worked free, dropped into the water and disappeared.

He must have disappeared himself very soon after.

· · · · · ·

With that sentence, that first day, I entered the pages of Pfaff's notebook. Thus are we linked, he and I. I use his pencil that had rolled off the table.

· · · · · ·

The house sits on a rise in the midst of trees, the pond glints through a web of bare branches. At this distance the clumps of reeds around its borders are hatchings against a grey wash, the wash of water against the lighter grey wash of the sky. In the distant background a dark mass of low hills. I stare at it through the pane as a prisoner might a remembered, an imagined landscape, so desired, so unattainable that, should I step outside this dreary cabin, it would forever recede no matter how persistently I followed it.

· · · · · ·

I'm leaving everything just as it was, gummy knife, apple core, cheese rind. I've simply added myself to the clutter of the place as though I were just another in Pfaff's collection of dried pods and cones, useless and incomprehensible as the meat baster on the floor. Except for this treadmill of words.

· · · · · ·

That ridiculous argument that day in Amsterdam coming out of the Rijksmuseum. I became quite exercised over the *Stillevens*, such a euphemism, so murky mercantile, I fumed, those dead rabbits, those braces of pheasants spotted with ruby gore, fixed in varnish rather than jelly, that's not life, still or otherwise, it's death in life, I said. All to glut the eye, the pride, the appetite, at the human table. And what of the worm's table? The Latins had it right, *nature morte*, *natura morta*, *naturaleza muerta*.

But she, with that deep, throaty laugh that assorted so oddly with her tiny frame, she insisted, quite triumphantly in the end, that, on the contrary, far from a euphemism, it's the aesthetic ideal. Fruit and flowers, flesh and feathered creatures, cut, or killed, at their most vital instant, their moment of highest bloom and vigor, no more to rot and wither, and so beyond process and death's decay. Isn't that what art does; in its beautiful incorruptibility it still lives, Henry, don't you see, it lives! She wore that day a suit she had made for travel out of a heavy dark rose cotton, narrow in the sleeves, clipped to the waist with a bell shaped skirt that had the stiff formality of an infanta.

· · · · · ·

The poor objects on this table are fixed in no tangled paradox, they continue quietly to decay whether I leave them there or throw them out. And Pfaff, the spirit of Pfaff, what of his nature? He haunts this place like some tormented ghost who cannot change or die.

Paula, Paula, what of you?

· · · · · ·

I prowl around the cabin like a creature caged. It's not my habitat. I sniff at everything, nuzzle it, turn it over. And so I came to look with attention at the drawings on the wall, wildflowers in ink and watercolor. Unremarkable enough, decorous renderings of his gleanings in the fields, careful and unremarkable but for one peculiarity. He's labeled them all with their common names, and then he's signed each one, not with a neat little cursive Pfaff as one would expect from the notebook, but with signatures full of an exasperated, puerile humor: Milkweed by Milksop, Phlox by Flux, Great Ragweed by Lesser Snotrag, Henbit by Henpecked, Vetch by Quetch, Madder by You Don't, and so on. I took them down and put them on the shelf with the other papers. It wouldn't do to expunge Pfaff's presence altogether, not that I could, but I don't mind clearing a little empty space for myself. Around myself.

．　．　．　．　．　．

Nights restless, in and out of sleep, dreams that drug rather than refresh. Ears pillow-muffled against the cacophony of waking birds I lie, furry mouth and rubbery limbs, stupefied until well past ten, until one or the other of those sacs that rule us, the one collapsed and contracting in spasms, the other painfully distended, forces me forth, feet tingling as though stuck with needles on the cold floor. The one now emptied, soon to refill, the other temporarily assuaged with coffee and a stale bun, I look without looking at the pond growing daily more obscure under the greening leaves. Each day has to be wound up like a mechanical toy. By late morning when the fog without and the funk within have lifted, I fling myself at the distant hills.

．　．　．　．　．　．

What did, does, Ellen hold against me? I haven't seen or heard from her since we faced each other across the table in that dreary parlor, the table that held the little cardboard box, and she looked at me with such venom as though I had planted the tumor in her mother's brain. Then turned without a word and hurried away. Me! as though I was ever able to plant anything in Paula!

．　．　．　．　．　．

The word breaks to silence.

．　．　．　．　．　．

The only human being I encounter on my walks is my neighbor, the old woman across the pond. She appears, suddenly, silently, out of nowhere, standing beside a bush on long stork-like legs. She has a frail fierce look, a *noli me tangere* ramrodness that a touch might topple. Paula was like that. We barely greet each other.   She seems as little inclined to company as I.

Hers is the only other house on the pond, not far distant by water, but by road a longish way around. I had to go there the first day to call the repairman about the water pump. A cabin small and dark like this one but closer to the water's edge and surrounded with thick brush. She came to the door, an emaciated creature, and looked at me with eyes wary, weary and fierce, the eyes of someone who has kept watch all night in a place full of enemies and is tired to the bone of it. She invited me in, found the name of the only repairman in the village, advised me how to deal with him and bade me goodbye with an utter indifference.

·　·　·　·　·　·

Looking for a pencil to continue these jottings I discovered in the table drawer a drawing pad containing a series of plant sketches, all under the rubric "False."　There was False Indigo, False Solomon's Seal, False Foxglove, False Hellebore, False Loosestrife, False Boneset, False Dragonhead. Could he have found all these falsities in his woods? Certain words underlined savagely with a black pen, all the Falses, then Seal and Glove and Hell, Loose and Strife and Bone.　You could read this whole excursus as encapsulating some scene of conflict and betrayal, played out, in true Elizabethan practice, with the emblems of flowers. Loosestrife—let loose the dogs of war; loose woman, that old debate as to what Hamlet thought Polonius meant when he said "I'll loose my daughter on him."

After the False series a section given over to various *Lysimachia*, the Yellow Loosestrife, *vulgaris*, *terrestris*, *nummularia*.　What is all this about? But these are not the true loosestrife since they do not belong to the Loosestrife Family, the *Lythryaceae*, but rather to the Primrose Family, the *Primulaceae*. Is there any significance to this confusion of families? Why in this instance only did he use the botanical rather than the common name? Lysimachus occurred to me, Alexander's general who was said to have, at the instigation of his wife, murdered his own son. Did Pfaff have a son? Or perhaps a daughter?

· · · · · ·

Came across Pfaff's boat, overturned and nearly hidden in the long grass by the edge of the pond. A flat bottom rowboat that doesn't look too much the worse for having spent a winter out of doors. I managed to turn it over and drag it closer to the water, and went up and got the oars that almost brained me the day I arrived, they had been left tipsily leaning against the back door, thinking, why not, I could launch it, in a foolish kind of excitement, a man in his early sixties who never learned to swim, but with the exertion the excitement palled and I left it there, nose in the pond. I hope it doesn't rain.

· · · · · ·

Paula was sewing for a small repertory company when we met in the reference room of my library. She had come to gather material for a production of *Love's Labour's Lost*, and I helped her, heaven help me.   The ironies in this don't escape me. A diminutive woman, leafing through an enormous folio of prints, a face still young but already ravaged, hair drawn tightly back into a coil on the top of her head, an almost regal stance, luminous grey eyes.   Hands, I noticed her hands, small and blunt, practiced, competent hands. They dealt with the heaviest, the stiffest, the most recalcitrant stuffs — upholstery stuffs, curtain stuffs — they wrestled big bolts onto the table, wielded heavy shears with complete certitude, stretched and pulled and puckered and stitched, while the frown lines deepened and the throaty caressing laugh would break out.

Why she took up with me I never understood. Her friends were struggling actors, potters, weavers, impecunious painters, that sort of thing; excessive, full of pretense, not unlike the Loosestrife Family one could say, but warm and congenial, almost familial. Paula liked that.   They soon learned not to expect anything from me; it didn't bother them, I was part of the backdrop. As for Ellen, Paula's child, she sized up our situation with the same unerring, I should say merciless, judgment that her mother used to cut into an ell of cloth.   And found it to her distaste. I was fifteen years Paula's senior; I had no illusions. What little I could have I took.

· · · · ·

I've deliberately <u>not</u> turned back Pfaff's written pages in this notebook, a patent inconsistency, since nothing keeps me from examining his pictures. Why? Because they are objects in a way words are not? Less revealing? More revealing? In any case last night I came upon another strange discovery. You might almost think he left these things around on purpose, for someone to stumble on. The nights are cool, they're long too, and I went to get some paper from the box on the back stoop to wad into the stove. Found another drawing pad. No flower pastels this time. Page after page of a monstrous creature, a thick black grub with bulging eyes, six legs covered with bristles, an enormous scoop in place of a mouth. A hairy face, nightmarishly enlarged. He drew this creature from many angles and with exactness of detail. Underneath, the legend: The Nymph Hagenius. Ye Gods!

· · · · · ·

How would I describe myself? A quiet, retired, retiring man with a modest competence, the second of Paula's husbands, a man of late middle years who expected to predecease her, a step-father steeped in scorn, one who prefers the anonymity of cities, a person given to enthusiasms followed by apathies, low tonus, middling energies, prone to doubt, one on whom the past weighs, an ex-librarian specialized in Renaissance studies, that most useless of living creatures, a second-rate dealer in others' lives and words. What am I doing here, alone in this rough cabin? The dried spores of alien lives. What if Pfaff should appear, bearded, with leaf-matted hair? What would I say to him? What would he say to me?

· · · · · ·

Winds and rain, and in the leaf litter frail white flowers veined in pink. I came upon my neighbor in the woods; she was holding one by the stem. "A spring beauty," she said to me as though we were continuing the conversation we never started, "one of the ephemerals," and she held it out to me. "It won't last more than a day."

· · · · · ·

A mystery resolved. Under the bed, along with clots of dust, balled-up socks, mine among them, hence the search, a small book, copiously underlined, enchantingly illustrated, with pictures in colors of iridescent beauty of that long-bodied stick-pin insect we named as children, and fled from with half-believing screams, the darning needle. Each one clings singly to reed or blade of grass, the bodies enameled in deep greens, blues, red, black, or shot with gold, each in its brilliance and simplicity, its stillness, with an intense reality. What have we here? A book on the Order of the *Odonata*, with its two sub-orders, the *Anisoptera* or Dragonfly and its more delicate relative, the slender *Zygoptera* or Damselfly. Our horrendous friend, *Hagenius*, is nothing more than the nymph or larva, 3/4 of an inch long, of a rapacious and common dragonfly species, thick-bodied, horned and hairy, who eats his kind if he can get it, a crawler and a sprawler in the mud of streams and ponds. The frontispiece photo, in black and white, I find extraordinarily moving. A young man in knickers and wading boots, looking across a reed-fringed pond with a face of immaculate calm.

A loose page fell out of the book. A page torn from a notebook, in Pfaff's small hand. Something he copied? The beginning of an essay?

The Toothed Ones

Every year for the past 350 million years the dragonfly has returned to the streams and bogs. Perhaps in the beginning, in the warm humidity of the Cambrian, when the immense insect, the largest ever known, lumbered through giant ferns on three foot wings, before there were seasons, the type was continually present. We have no evidence of his larval stage; only the splendor of the winged fossil form etched in stone.

Today he is little changed from this ancestral Megisoptera; only much reduced in size and capable of dazzling speed. His passage is brief and scintillating; all color and motion, delicacy and ferocity. There are those who have believed he bears on his back the souls of the dead . . .

•　•　•　•　•　•

Sun up at noon, I have taken to stretching out on the wharf, belly down, head hanging over the water. The pond, black and turbid, a dark glass in which I see not only not clearly, I see not at all. It gives up nothing of the murderous dramas of its depths whose tale I have just read, the assassin's stalk, the victim's flight. Peaceable and bland, it reflects from its mirroring surface only that which is without, shadows of passing clouds or birds, images of reed or branch, my own distorted wavering face across which, supported by the liquid tension of the water, floats a leaf, a feather, the sheet of paper that I tore from Pfaff's notebook and tossed in. It will waterlog, and go to join the thread-like worm.

So much for reflections on or from the pond.

You Nymphs Called Naiads

The torn page, nonporous bond, bearing Pfaff's close script, floated on the surface of the pond, too light to break the surface tension of the water. It circled sluggishly in the random currents. Gradually the seep of water lay a thin glaze over the letters; the scrap of paper turned on its edge and slowly sank. On the muddy bottom it came to rest against a clump of stems.

The tiny slits in the reed stems that Pfaff had noted would scar over once "the threadlike worm" wriggled loose from the egg and dropped into the water. Within minutes the minute thing cast its first cuticle; thus freed, the body began to expand, the legs spread out, and a gas replaced the liquid in its breathing tubes. By the third molt, it had consumed the yolk sac in its gut and had become, technically speaking, a nymph, or more precisely, as water-dweller, a naiad. Tiny, weak, rudimentary, it crawled among the reeds and hid.

Ten cast-off casings, each larger than the last, marked its growth. The six legs lengthened and articulated; the wing sheaths, close against the body and presently useless, enlarged, and with each molt the globular eyes covered an ever greater expanse of head, new facets at the front pushing the older ones toward the rear. What began as several hundred ommatidia finished in the thousands. It wore its hinged prehensile lower lip folded up over its face like a mask.

Many others like to this had fallen into the water from the stems of *Potogomaton*. For several summers they dawdled in the forest of stalks, molting repeatedly until the onset of winter put a stop to it and in a state of suspension they waited for spring. In their early instars they were pale green striped with brown, as though they too had been a reed; grown swift and lithe and strong with powerful jaws they turned somber, having no more need of camouflage. They would become that *Anax* Pfaff had watched, the bronze-green beauty of the air.

Others came to people the pond differently. She who had walked down and then up the reed punching neat holes with the sharp tool at her tail and inserting in each an egg had worked alone. But there a couple hung above the water clasped together in tandem lock. He released her and hovering waited and watched as, silvered in a film of air, she climbed down beneath the water to bury her eggs in elodea's soft green leaves. An hour she lingered at great risk for what might come cleaving the wave to snap her up. When she came to the surface he clasped her below the head and drew her up and flew her off again. The naiad that hatched grew slender and small and made her summer home among the fernlike leaves and stems of the floating plant; Enallagma she was called.

Like Anax, the beautiful widow Libellus Luctuosa,

in weeds of black, flew to the pond unattended. With the tip of her abdomen she struck the water again and again, releasing her thousands. Some sifted to the bottom silt, encased in a jelly that grafted them to the pond floor. There they hatched, the ugly offspring, dark, stout and hairy, to squat, sullen and slothful, in the black ooze.

Even deeper buried in the mud lay some like crocodiles with but the tip of eyes and tails to mark their presence. Should soft small larva of biting midge or gnat crawl or swim past, their antennae would quiver to the faint vibrations and out would shoot the enormous scoop to snatch it up. So they would feed and cast their skins and grow and years might pass before ever they were prompted to depart.

Throughout the day the damsel nymph Enallagma pressed motionless against a stem in the tangled mat of vegetation, hiding in the mottled reflections of the clouds. From the upper world a steady debris filtered to the pond floor. A morsel of torn white paper slowly twisting nudged her as it sank. Threatened she slid around the stem to the opposite side and jerked her abdomen toward her head, pointing her tail fins in a futile gesture of defense. So for some time she remained before she could relax into her customary immobility.

For the pond was dangerous. Beneath the placid surface waters scenes were enacted from a Boschian hell. A giant scavenger beetle chopped up a naiad's headless torso with its powerful jaws; a back strider pierced its victim with beak-like mouth and sucked the juices; the dark sleek forms of trout or bream slipped past with open gullet, winnowing. Not least to fear, if she could know or fear, would be her own cannibal kind.

But the dragonfly nymph Anax hunted actively all the day, bulging eyes alert to every movement. Water streaking through his anal gills jetted him after the fleeing ceratopognid whose snakelike wriggle couldn't save it; through clumps of reeds he climbed catlike to stalk and pounce on what would no more become mosquito or beetle or stone fly. A voracious eater, even in darkness he took no rest, for then he left the upper reaches to hunt on the pond floor. Lurking behind Pfaff's paper blind, he waited to leap out upon whatever swam past.

Enallagma had already abandoned the safety of her perch to creep downward where she could hunt under shield of darkness. Nearer and nearer Anax's blind she came, all unsuspecting. She swam with a peculiar undulating gait, paddling with her legs and fluttering the three leaf-like gills at her tail.

With his small antennae Anax picked up the vibrations of her approach. His large head pivoted and training his enormous eyes in their direction he waited. When, as in the crosshairs of a gun, the visual axes of the two eyes intersected, at the precise distance between victim and lower lip, he struck. Out shot the lip, two hooked claws seized her around the middle and the whole apparatus retracted pulling her wriggling to his mouth. The powerful mandibles did the rest. Nothing was wasted. Bits that fell onto the lip as he chewed he retrieved till all was consumed. The tool that served as pincers, fork and table he folded neatly against his face. Flexing it again in and out, he lifted a leg to clean his mouth and scratch his head and took up once more his patient motionless wait.

Then the muck began to heave and fall away. A fearsome head rose from the mire, a body, blunt and hairy, crawled forth on ponderous legs. Antennae bristles stiffened to detect the least excitement of the water. But it was Anax, immobile behind his blind, who picked up instead the oscillations of the monster's approach. Ignorant of what was drawing near he made himself ready.

Onward came Gomphus in slow relentless course. Anax, the swift, might easily have swum away but he did not mean to lose his vantage point and his territory. He set his sights and as the creature came within range rushed forth and struck him with his armed lip. Gomphus, startled, humped back and bending sideways jerked his abdomen above his head; his anal spines opened and shut threateningly. Anax swung at him with lifted abdomen and stabbed him with violent thrusts of his sharp spines. Spun off balance the heavy naiad fell on his side. Anax, the agile, keeping out of reach of the powerful jaw, darted in and grabbed him by the tail. The monster struggled to right himself; with the other clinging tight he pulled himself free and fled to his lair, leaving behind in the victor's grasp, like Grendel's arm, his anal paraproct.

So Anax lived into the summer, and at each instar, without his cognizance, the wing sheaths swelled to make room for the wings that grew within, folded accordion style, against the day they should unfurl in air. In the final stage, there were strange unsettling changes. His eyes darkened and spread across his head; within three weeks they had met in the center. The formidable weapon of the lower lip shrunk to uselessness and the greedy animal now must pass days at fast. Gills ceased to absorb oxygen from the water but the need for oxygen to fuel these changes was great and soon Anax with many others might be seen hanging half out of water, breathing through newly-opened holes in the thorax, breathing, that is, air.

Every so often migratory impulses swept the pond. In the spring the hairy nymphs burrowed in mud rose in their multitudes and stiff-legged and awkward headed toward the warm shallows close to shore. By summer the weed dwellers had begun to climb to the surface vegetation. On a late warm June afternoon, Anax, spurred by hormonal promptings, left the water. He climbed a *Potomogeton*, that same reed from which, a minute speck, he had first dropped into the pond. He gripped the reed with his tarsal claws and wriggled violently from side to side. The support held. He clung there motionless. Only the obscurity of dusk shielded him from merciless sharp eyes, avid beaks. Now was the moment of considerable danger.

Letters

Dear Beatrice,

I have to apologize for the abrupt end to our talk last night. This place is in a '30s time warp; one of its charms no doubt. First the operator couldn't get a circuit and then that infernal din. The phone hangs behind an ancient cash register, the kind that jangles like a fire alarm when it opens and business that night was booming. All the males around Hopbottom were hanging out at Ed's General Store. With all that racket I could scarcely hear you but I thought I understood you to say it would be all right for me to stay on longer.

Would you please let me know as soon as possible. Something has come up and which really requires that I stay a while longer.

Have you news of Pfaff? I thought I understood you to say that he wouldn't be returning any time soon. I don't mean to pry but I wonder if you know his plans or whereabouts.

I can't tell you how grateful I am to you for offering me this place, to a practical stranger. I realize you do this for Paula's sake. A propos, have you heard from Ellen, do you keep in touch?

Yours,
Henry

Dear Beatrice,

Thank you for answering so promptly. So I did hear you agree to my staying longer and I'm delighted and most grateful.

Up to now I pretty much left things as I found them. I don't know if you've been here since Pfaff left but things were lying around in quite a chaos and I was reluctant to disturb anything not knowing when or whether he might return, and feeling, to be honest, like an intruder, but on the other hand, grateful that I could simply light on top of things like a fly leaving no imprint, except of course the microbial spread of disease.

If I understood you it appears unlikely that Pfaff is coming back any time soon. So I'll go ahead now and pack some of the stuff he left lying around. I won't throw anything out unless it's manifestly garbage. In fact I'll make an inventory. It's the librarian in me, some of this has intrinsic interest.

In fact, I don't mean to be gossipy, but he's an altogether intriguing character. They don't have much good to say about him in the village; he kept to himself. On those infrequent times he came out from his woods to get his supplies he wouldn't give you the time of day, grudging of speech, gruff in answer. Every now and then he'd show up at the tavern, seat *himself in a corner downing beer after beer, so grim and silent no one dared approach him, until something would set him off, some chance word overheard perhaps, and he'd start to rave and make such a fracas that it took two strong men finally to get him out the door.*

I'm enclosing another 3-month's rent.

Yours,

Henry

Emergence

This letter I would write to Pfaff:

Surely you would find this strange, this letter from someone whose existence you ignore, moreover an interloper in your house. Where are you anyway and do you even exist? But to whom could I tell this but to you, Pfaff, although you'll never see this. Who else would understand, you in your own way otherwise crazy?

I was bumping around in your rowboat down at the pond, keeping to the edges, mapping the contours, as it were. It was one of those spacious days, full of glisten and hum and the varying beats of time, the boat barely moving in the current, the air quick with wings. I'd gone into one of those half-states of attention, scarcely even using the oars, just enough to keep from getting snagged in the debris of limbs and roots, and trailing a hand through water dark and cool and rank with a green ferny weed that floated like a mat on the surface. I pulled up a handful of the stuff. Something was clinging to a stem, brown, about an inch long. Looking closely I could make out the crook of legs, hair-thin, a segmented body, a blunt head, bulging eyes. It didn't move and I took it home and put it, fern and all, into a jar with water. It was, as you will certainly have guessed, I've seen your drawings, a damsel nymph.

I left it there on the table by the window. After

a few days I noticed it had climbed up the stem out of the water. It clung there for several days without moving and of course without eating; I wouldn't have known what to feed it. I thought it had probably died and pretty much forgot about it. But early one morning I was standing by the window watching the trees at the pond walk out of the mist and I happened to glance at the jar. And there in a strange embrace, around the spiny legs that grasped the stem another set of legs were clasped, and half hanging from the split shell another creature clung, with damp crumpled wings. It hung there for I don't know how long.

I watched, in a state now of quite extraordinary excitement; at last it bent forward and grasped the shell with its legs and slowly pulled the rest of its long narrow body free. The wings began to open up and stiffen; pale, delicate, beautiful; it was a marvel, this winged creature that had come to me out of the jar.

When the wings began to flutter I was afraid it would hurt itself and I took it, jar and all, to the edge of the pond but first I marked it on the back with a yellow pen (I learned that in one of your books). Near the place where I had found it I opened the jar. It had crawled to the top of the stem, the glassy wings were pulsating as though they sensed freedom and the light breeze. I shook it loose. I thought it might fall to the ground but it lifted and flew to the nearest twig and there it clung for minutes helpless and exposed. "Go," I said.

"Go." At last it decided for flight and on wavering wings made for the woods and was gone. I know it sounds crazy but when it flew off something hit me like a blow in the gut.

Then began a strange affair. For now the pond was rife with dragonflies; mid morning they would begin to arrive and by noon the air was thick with them, whirring and darting and perching on reeds. I took to spending long mornings by the water, sitting on the boat moored and slightly rocking. Your binoculars came in handy, your books too, especially Needham; I began to be pretty good at identifying dragonflies, the more obvious species of course. There was a whole cast of them: the big green *Anax*, a brilliant red *Somatochlora*, one splendid creature with turquoise head and greenish-blue banded body, one with white and brown brindled wing, a *Libellula pulchella*, the Blue Pirate, *Pachydiplax longipennis*, the white-faced Belted Skimmer. But down deep I was always hoping, hoping *she* might come, the one I had dotted with yellow. That she was a *she* I took for granted; the name perhaps, or some other sense of things. I knew it was foolish. More than likely, in that weak tender stage you people call teneral she'd been caught and eaten by a bird or spider or one of her own cannibalistic kind. She was so new to this world above water; how did she even know how to fly? Still she knew enough to hide among the trees until her body grew hard and brilliant and the wings took on their full strength and span.

And then one day in the lower passages of the air, working close to shore, I saw a slender needle-like creature flit restlessly, perch and flit and perch again quite near me on a reed. The cobalt body stretched into the air like a furled flag or an enameled pin, the gauzy wings were folded and upraised, and on the thorax, above the juncture of the wings, my mark—my yellow spot. I didn't dare move; I held my breath, afraid to startle her, in terror that she fly away.

Does that seem exaggerated? It is. It surely is. And that's why I'm writing you. I'm sure this would never happen to you. You observe; you don't transgress, except perhaps with words.

The Damselfly

We meet every day. Once the sun has burned off the morning mists and risen high enough to warm the wings for flight she comes. I wait, seated in the rowboat, Pfaff's torn straw hat pulled down on my forehead, my hands, slightly trembling, tensed on the oars. The noon sun scalds my back through my thin shirt and scorches my bare arms; the water, like a glass, gathers the rays and throws them into my face; my eyes dazzle. She comes fluttering, weaving and bobbing along the shore to perch nearby on the same elastic reed. Joy overtakes me, intense as the joy of childhood. She perches long minutes, wings blue-brilliant now, clapped together and held high; I watch, still as any stone.

If she does not come where I am posted, I grow impatient and scout around the periphery of the pond. These excursions are inevitably fruitless; I return and wait, and, as though by assignation, in time she will return to that same spot, and bask in the sun upon that very reed.

This has become the pattern of the days. Accident? Or design?

So today, instead of taking my usual post I hid behind a low bush near the shore. The sun rose, dragonflies in their multitudes swooped and whirled. The reed stayed empty beside the empty boat. A dark thick dragon briefly perched, set the reed swaying, flew off again; another skimmed by, blue and green; it was not she. By noon there was still no sign of her. I hurried to the boat; there was a madness of insects in the air. I took the boat and worked it gently around the edges of the pond. There were others like her flitting and darting; no sooner did I draw near one that perched than it shot into the air to alight further on, always out of reach, and on none could I distinguish the yellow dot I had marked her with and made her mine.

The next day. Cloudy; only a few insects fluttering sluggishly. I wait till noon; still no sign of her. I seek her in the woods. They are in there somewhere, wings folded, hiding, waiting for sun. I stumble around, peering under stones and logs, in the crooks of twigs, kicking the leaf litter, cursing the miserable doubting curiosity that broke the frail link between us.

Day three: the sun is up; the people of the pond are all about, an explosion of activity. It's a kind of madness; flights, pursuits, gyrations; they whirl around me as though I were a log, a stone, as though I didn't exist, so close I could hear the wing whirr. I close my eyes; I can't bear it. When I open them again, she is there.

She is there; that ends experiments. Day after day I take my place at the appointed time and always she comes and sits quietly beside me. So Paula and I would sit for hours at an outdoor cafe in the Trastevere mesmerized by the noisy goings on of a neighborhood that made the piazza its living room.

The pond is their village; I watch them, in their comings in and goings out. I watch her; she flies off, she comes back, she has been hunting. She carries her food in the spiny basket of her legs; she will sit on her perch and dine. I have watched her ablutions, she combs the dust and cobwebs off her eyes and face with her brushy legs, tips up her tail to clean between her wings.

A thick-bodied black Gomphus whirs past like a helicopter. He wears blue bands like some ungainly overbearing policemen. I get up, waving my arms and shouting, as though either of them could hear. He comes up behind her and in a flash she is off. The Gomphus patrols importantly on, hovering on antic wings. It is some time before she returns to her perch.

Elodea dots the pond with small cuplike blossoms, yellow-centered. An orb web is strung in a corner to catch the unwary. A damsel flies safely under it but another has been caught and is vainly struggling. The black spider at the center waits. It is a cannibal world, rife with dangers. I've seen a Dragon hunter catch and devour a Sympetrum. I've seen the wings that the birds spat.

Here one has stretched her body out like a flag and is curving the tip down seductively, an invitation. He dances up and down before her, seizes her head in his forelegs, carries her off. Curling his long abdomen up and over with the agility of an acrobat he lets go of his grip, and clasps her neck instead with his anal paraprocts, the two blades

41

at the tip, that fit so neatly into their preordained niches, or out she'd toss him. He flies her to a perch, he has a vital preliminary to take care of. He presses his end against his middle, taking momentarily the form of a figure eight, as he transfers the sperm from the anal opening to the rather fearful-looking hooked organ located just beneath the wings (at the venter of abdominal segment no. 2). This accomplished, with little stroking encouragements he induces her to bend her body up and press its tip, her little purse, against him; as she clings to him with her claws they take their nuptial flight slowly across the pond, a wheel, a heart, a harp. And he, the sly troubadour, carefully moves aside the clump of sperm left by the last suitor so that *his* will take the prize, the clutch of eggs. At least so says Waage, no wag he.

And how do they know that? *Footnote 12. In the following experiment males copulating with tethered females are kept in copula by decapitation with a dissecting scissors.* The engaged genitalia with segments of the abdomen were cut away and dissected and thus the mystery of sperm transfer was disclosed.

Guiding her now to a bending reed he hovers protectively for a while as she walks methodically down the blade, inserting into each little slit she makes with her sharp tail a row of eggs. A passing female catches his eye, forgetful of his paternal responsibilities he flies off in hot pursuit, leaving his damsel half immersed in water. She continues her trek down the blade until she is completely submerged, at the mercies of what might come; a frog, a newt, a fish, a water scorpion, a diving beetle, a belostomatid bug. When at last she surfaces, water logged, another grasps her head and pulls her out of the water and carries her aloft to mate in mid-air. But she will not, or cannot, cooperate; he drops her into the water with a thud. The poor bedraggled thing paddles to the nearest reed and climbs wearily out. I think of some Dickensian waif at two in the morning on a cold windy deserted London street, clutching her tattered shawl around her.

A blue pair whirls by in tandem; they settle on a leaf. But something is amiss in the boudoir. She does not bend her abdomen toward him compliantly but holds her long pointed self stiff and straight. For some reason he does not please her. Or maybe she has had enough. He lets her go. Not every reluctant female gets off so easily. I saw one getting slapped around by her suitor; another pulled out of the water where she was laying her eggs and when she wouldn't mate he ate her. It was risky anyway, the tandem act. I saw a tandem couple harassed by a bunch of toughs trying to separate them; another perched pair caught and eaten by a grasshopper

Last night I found among Pfaff's papers an article describing experiments in a wind tunnel, attempts to unravel the mysteries of dragonfly flight. That night this dream:

I am walking down to the pond in the early

morning. It is a scene of mayhem, the reeds along the bank trampled down and muddy, all life gone but for a few insects lying on the ground with broken wings, bodies in the water. I know at once what has happened, a gang has come and captured them, she too. I set out after them, following a trail of bodies across hills and woods and city streets until I come to a large brick building with no windows. Inside are corridors and men in white suits scurrying, but none would stop to speak to me. I come to a door. Hanging on a string is a tandem pair, one dead and headless but holding the other, still struggling. I open the door. Inside men in white suits holding notebooks stand around a large metal tunnel. I see some of the pond folk tethered by strings hanging from their heads, and she among them. A stocky man in black stands by ready to pull the switch. I try to cry out "Stop" but no sound comes; he turns, I know him, it is Pfaff. I never saw eyes so cold. "Restrain him," he says, "he is obscuring knowledge," and when I try to fling myself on him, my arms are pinned behind me. I hear a roar of wind and the sound of soundless screams.

I wake in a clutch of panic.

The sun was high that morning before I got to the pond, half dreading a scene of carnage or worse — instead, a bacchanalia. The air filled with wheeling couples, one and all touched by Eros' wand, by libidinous frenzy ta'en, compelled to replicate their kind. Was she among them? I couldn't tell. She wasn't at her reed. It was quite beautiful, this slow dance of circled, lazily circling bodies, wings throwing off sun sparkles, as unaware as the dancers on the Titanic, for in a few weeks they would all be gone. A dance of life. A dance of death.

The Mouth Of Truth

I am in a state of shock. Beatrice was here! exuding perspiration and worry. She had walked up from the village. I hurried to the kitchen to get her some water and pull myself together. I don't like invasions. When I came back she was prowling around examining the drawings on the walls. Mercifully the bedroom door was closed.

Pfaff's, I said. In case she might think they were mine. Is he coming back? I asked, afraid that's what had brought her here.

But it wasn't. She still hasn't heard from him. In fact she's beginning to worry. She hopes nothing has happened.

It took her some time to get to the point. The point being that she had found something in a drawer, something Paula had left with her years ago and she had completely forgotten, and now, full of apologies, she had come to give it to me. Couldn't she have mailed it? She was probably hoping I'd open it and let her see what was inside. She fished it out of that familiar bulging reticule and handed it to me. A large envelope. It had Paula's name on it and was sealed by tape. So I laid it on the table. And asked her if she wanted some tea.

She didn't want tea. She wanted to explain. I hate explanations. She steamrolled on. So I learned about the drawer in the guest room where she kept extra linens, those seldom used, probably hadn't been used since Paula stayed there when she was having the baby. Before she left to move up north Paula asked to leave this envelope with her until she called for it. She said there were papers in it she didn't want to have but she didn't want to lose either. Beatrice was sure it had to do with that unfortunate business which, by the way, she knew almost nothing about since Paula never wanted to talk about it, and what should she do, pry? There was gossip of course, and rumors, you know what theatre people are. Paula finally wrote she'd found a little house and was taking in dressmaking so she could be home with the baby but she never mentioned the envelope, and there it lay all these years, forgotten.

At long last, disappointed no doubt in her curiosity and just as she was going out the door she turned and asked me casually if I had heard from Ellen. Not recently I said, not wanting her to know I never hear from Ellen. She's had her baby, B. said. Baby? I said stupidly. Yes, of course, B said, that's why Paula went to London, to get her to stop it.

She's all alone. Beatrice said. I think she wants to come home.

I have an excited imagination. Was that her mission? To prepare me for Ellen's return? With child? Where does Pfaff come in? Or does he come in? There's Beatrice sitting in her corner like a fat benignant spider, tweaking on the threads. What is her involvement in all this –- with Paula who went to her to have her child? with Ellen, with whom she's obviously still in touch? with Pfaff, the man of mystery? with getting me here? For what mysterious purpose? Why?

Took a long walk to clear my head.

There's that big envelope, lying on the table. I'm the opposite of curious. I don't really want to know. Never have. Never asked. Was never told. Am tempted to throw the thing in the garbage.

No, I'm opening it.

Letters, and pictures.

A photograph, black and white: three people, two men and a woman. The woman is tiny, her hair is long, she is young, she is smiling. It is Paula. They're all smiling. One of the men, the shorter of the two, has on a checked shirt, open at the neck with a military jacket unbuttoned over it; he looks older than the others, his hair is beginning to recede, a brotherly arm is laid across Paula's shoulder; the taller one has a military cap cocked jauntily; he is smiling broadly with all his teeth, big square teeth. He's athletic, broad-shouldered, a good-looking Nordic type. He leans on the hood of a convertible; behind is sky and sea.

Letters. Three in a hand so sprawling it seems to want to fill up space without saying anything, an adolescent unformed hand, these are signed George. George, I surmise, is the tall blond. He's home, unhappy, misses her, everything about his old life seems changed; he hasn't told his parents yet, he's waiting for the right moment, etc. etc. In the next letter he rambles on about how he's spending his time, just going through the motions of sailing and tennis and swimming and parties while all the while he's thinking of her, but the right moment hasn't come and in a postscript he advises her not to write to that address; the last letter is short and cryptic: they know, they're furious.

A letter from Fred, perhaps the one with the brotherly arm. He describes a weekend at George's family compound in Nantucket, the moonlight sails, tennis quartets, dances at the club, clam bakes, pretty girls all buzzing around George. He's in his element, old George. Fred appears unaware of the impending drama, or is this a subtle forewarning? Do we know what kind of cad we're dealing with?

There's a long envelope from a law firm. This letter informs her that the family has turned the matter over to him, the lawyer; that the son, being underage, and she being 10 years older, they are seeking an annulment on the grounds of entrapment, that the son has given his consent and it would therefore be in her best interest not to contest it, and when the proper papers were issued she would be notified. This letter was dated October; Ellen was born the following May; Paula would have been several months pregnant at the time. Did he know? Did they? Did she put up a fight?

Beneath the pile is another letter, not from George or Fred; Paula has sent it. But it's come back, unopened; on the envelope an emphatic hand has written: Address unknown. Return to Sender. The date's smudged over, can't read it.

I had to struggle with myself to open it. She had been told not to write; she had written. Desperation? I underestimated Paula's intransigent pride. The envelope contained a postcard. Nothing was written on it. I turn it over and am startled by the image on the other side. It is a large circle in rough stone representing a human face with slits for eyes, a small hole for a nose, and a larger opening for a mouth, an archaic looking figure, as indeed it was, for it was an ancient Roman artifact christened the *Bocca della Verità*, the Mouth of Truth.

The *Bocca della Verità*. It had produced another of those arguments that dogged the trip so inaptly called our honeymoon, the year before Paula died.

It was our last day in Rome.

I wanted to see Michelangelo's *Moses*. Paula absolutely insisted that we go instead to this out of the way corner which took some hunting to find, a small piazza empty of tourists. On the porch of the church, early medieval, stood this huge marble disc, looking like an immense manhole, which in fact it probably had once been, a sewer drain cover, from early Roman times. The figure was arresting, more like some ancient river god than an arm of the ecclesia, something primitive and barbarous, and indeed sinister, considering the uses it was put to. It was called the *Bocca della Verità*; legend had it that if a liar put his hand in the mouth the mouth would snap closed. Husbands took their wives there to determine their fidelity. Paula said that the

Renaissance Popes used it as a conduit for anonymous calumnies and denunciations. I don't know where she got that idea.

That was her answer to him, had he the sense to read it. Which I doubt. And I guess to me too. Lilies that fester.

But still. *Moses*, as opposed to that fluvial manhole cover! Of course I had no idea why she had dragged me there, and irritation got the best of me. We argued there, on Santa Maria's porch, though I had to admit (privately) the early mosaics were quite beautiful, we argued on the way back, and the argument flared up again at dinner. Our last dinner in Rome. Too bad to spoil it. But I couldn't understand it; it was simply incommensurable! And she knew what store I set on seeing the Michelangelo. She could always run rings around me; so she did again, prating about the purity, the simplicity, the quiet of the ancient church, pointing out the lack of tourists, the virtue of going off the beaten track, and on and on, everything but the truth as I now realize, that she had to go scratch the scab on her feelings once again, after all the years.

Good god, Ellen coming home! Now.

Shorai-Tombo

. . . an old Japanese belief that certain dragonflies
are ridden by the dead

- Lafcadio Hearn

It is early September. I go, as is my wont, down
to the pond. The life there is noticeably calmer; the
frenzy of high summer fading to fall. A few of the
larger dragonflies are still around, their brilliant
colors dulled with age beneath a hoary bluish cast,
pruinose they call it, the white bloom on a plum.
They perch sluggishly on slightly rocking bending
reeds. Feeling a similar lassitude, I sit in my slightly
rocking boat, no longer expecting my lady would
appear. It has been some ten days now since I have
seen her.

The scene so familiar; the translucent pond
garlanded with reeds and the darker border of the
trees; the transected vision of the old woman
opposite, seated in profile in her wooden chair with
her head bent over the book in her lap, though I
never see her turn a page, and so she sits, and so
do I, somnolent.

Something flickers past my half closed eyes; one
of the perchers has left his reed and begun to climb
in figure eights into the upper air. It seems so
gratuitous, this flight, without cause or pyrotechnics,
just this steady ascent, higher and higher until it
vanishes into the white of the sky.

This air weighs. Heavy, exhausted. It's the days, the pile up of days, the days of summer. All withered now. The distance between the nodes on the reed is short. I read this somewhere. "A space short as the nodes of the reeds of Naniwa."

She is gone and *she* is gone and all must go. She of the glittery wings; she of the aloof air, the warm and husky voice. Fleeing before us, just beyond our grasp. And some will come.

Did that one get to puncture the green stem to bequeath her progeny before the frog devoured her? Or spider in his web? Or something gnawing? Time is short between the nodes. To me she was maiden, damsel, I have been beguiled by a name.

Beguiled indeed. By something other than a name.

A glimpse of movement on the opposite side of the pond, someone walking around the side of the house. The mailman perhaps. He comes to her where she sits with her back to him and her head bent over her book. He touches her on her shoulder, evidently thinking she sleeps, and slowly, as though in slow motion, she crumples. He tries to catch her around the body as she slides; he staggers under her weight as though they are a couple in some bizarre dance. He stretches her out on the lawn, he kneels, he touches her gingerly on the forehead, he looks around, frantic now, as if for help, he takes to his heels.

As in a dumb show. From where I sit, in the boat, I see her stretched and motionless form. I could pick up the oars and go to her.　　But why? Whatever gnawed at her, she wanted no interference. I sit. Something gnaws in me.

．　．　．　．　．　．

　　The woman, having knocked and received no answer, pushed the door ajar and stepped inside dragging her heavy suitcase behind her.　The baby nestled against her in a sling.　The room was empty, no one came in answer to her call.　She unhooked the sleeping infant and laid it on a table. The table was bare except for a pair of binoculars and a large dried-up insect which she brushed to the floor.
　　She sat and rested, waiting.　When the light changed she went to the window.　A uniform grey now covered the sky. The sun was gone. Through a gap in the trees she saw the pond dark and dully gleaming and at its very center, dwarfed by distance, a small boat idled.　With its oars dangling by its side, it drifted listlessly, bearing a seated figure in a broad brimmed hat, so still he seemed but a silhouette against the sky.
　　She picked up the binoculars.

‡

Ponte Vecchio

Ponte Vecchio

The imbroglio in the post office — yet another among life's minor humiliations.

Arthur Brown, his hair now white and thin, not a sign of that once rich earth-brown, sick, old, friendless, a foreigner, monolingual, and alone, moreover, his faculties going, the dead cells piled like scum along the edges of a shore, is pounding along as fast as trembling gait and weakened hams could take him through streets that grew in unfamiliarity the more he walked them. The sun already lay dying behind the dark ancient buildings when the old servant in the green apron had shuffled in with his single piece of mail. He had seized the yellow slip, or was it blue, no matter, his hands shaking, ears pulsing, had turned it over and over, and was finally brought to understand that this was not his letter, a letter was waiting for him at the central post office, a very important letter, signor, one that wishes a special care. It was Flossie, it could only be Flossie, answering him. His cry for help.

He stumbled up the stairs, bumped and jostled by people pushing past. The heavy doors swung back and forth in his face. He scurried into a large cold dim room with numbered windows from which depended lines of harried faces breathing in and out a used and acrid air. He was shunted from window to window, line to line, clerk to clerk. Finally the letter was taken from a cubbyhole, Flossie's childish scrawl barely visible under the cryptic markings of the rubber stamp. It approached his nose; his hand went out to receive it; then incredibly the letter drew away again, was returned to its niche, as the diffident and finally exasperated clerk explained in voluble Italian, crescendo, sustained by a chorus of grumbles behind him, that he couldn't have his letter without proving his identity, and the only acceptable proof of identity was the passport, not, sweeping them aside, these valueless documents (a superannuated driver's license, a frayed social security card, a Y membership). Even the residence permit wouldn't do. Though would the police have given him that without prior possession of a passport? This thought occurred to him later, but in any case he wouldn't have been able to express it. Identity, passport, these were the branches he clung to in this swirling flood of speech. Was he truly Mr. Arthur Brown? How could one be sure? The passport was in a drawer in his dingy little room on the other side of the river. Much too far. It was close to closing time.

Out in the street again, crowds and tumult. December's cold was in the air and early darkness. People eddied around the few fixed objects in their paths: the burly man with bulbous nose protuberant between hat and muffler tending the news kiosk, a black-shawled crone selling chestnuts at a smoking brazier; a death's head Punchinello in a booth shuffling lottery tickets. A trinity of ancients who never once looked at each other, nor did they throw a glance his way. The cars were out, throttling the city. A sluggish lumber and jam of machines that snorted, squealed, lunged, inched, backed and squeezed. Lights rippled from their shiny metal sides; white faces with agile eyes floated behind the glass; a rich glow of artificial energy, bitter fumes, a cacophony of horns.

He leaned against the blotched wall of the old building, his face blotched too, a paler wash on the porous masonry, and his body settled against the wall like a heavy bag of sand sifting downwards. The darkness, the moving lights, the power and menace of the cars confused him. He was no longer sure what direction to take. It was Flossie's doing; Flossie had sent him here. Deep down the engine of anger coughed, kicked over, died.

Sitting with Flossie in her hot little basement apartment in New York. On her burlapped walls glossy reproductions of sweet blond Virgins, youths with shapely calves and velvet cushions on their heads, the misty Tuscan landscape framed by crenulated arches. Her face round and earnest, pores exuding enthusiasm, eyes moist behind thick lenses, she is promising him an old age of leisure and pleasure in the storied city, its riches spread before him like a feast, etc. etc., his only duty to enjoy. What wouldn't she give to go herself? She works in the office of a large museum.

The three of them had a special interest in the city of Florence; it was, so to speak, Flossie's conceptive city. A pensione on the top floor of a decayed palazzo. Every morning at five the couple was wakened by the roar of Vespas, a clatter of carts and rumble of trucks, a hammering as booths went up. To this dissonant overture Flossie came into being. They would lean over the loggia balustrade to look on the marketplace below. The scene, so often dwelt upon, hung like a painting in their minds; the watchers on the balcony minute in one upper corner and below, lit by an early morning light, Ceres' colorful cornucopia heaped: tomatoes in huntsman's scarlet, burnt orange of persimmons, the vernal pale green of lettuce shading to the deep green of spinach and sheen of cucumber, eggplants gleaming blue-black, artichokes darkening to purple, coppery gold of oranges, yellow lemon glister.

Dresses on hangars swayed in the light breeze, sweaters, garish pinks and blues and greens, lay piled on tables. Gaudy balloons, pink and orange, bobbed aloft. Voices, laughter, filled the piazza. At one end the bare unfaced masonry of the church, its bell tower carved from a bright blue sky. Jean now dead, back he should go, back to this shared vision of felicity, though he was dubious about the five flights of stairs. The signora however didn't reply; the letter was returned, address unknown.

He went first to a place recommended by one of Flossie's colleagues. It was on a long treeless street with nondescript stone buildings, garages and machine shops, near the beltway that circled the city in the place of the old walls. After his heart attack he had to seek even cheaper quarters, and a male nurse at the hospital had found him a room in a steep narrow alley in the old part of town. But now he couldn't remember the name of the street, or even that of the tiny square nearby. Over a bridge. What bridge? On the other side of the river. A long way off.

The sagging sack began to firm. First, to leave the isle of safety, he must cross the dangerous stream of cars. Ahead of him the way was well-lit, bustling, full of folk; it was, he believed, the way he had come. The street to the side was dark, untraveled.

He hesitated for a long time at the curb. The traffic moved east when it moved but for long uncertain intervals it halted, and then the bold pedestrian would dart across, side–stepping, pushing at fenders. Without warning the pack of cars would surge forward again leaving some people perilously stranded in the middle. They went on chatting as though seated in their living rooms. Brown took the plunge with a near fatal error of judgment. One foot off the curb, in mid-air, just as the lights changed. Something huge, black and shiny bore down on him. He teetered, flailed his arms, grabbed at a woman next to him, clutching the handbag hanging from her shoulder. Brakes squealed, a livid face stared at him through the distorting glass, mouth contorted and working soundlessly, fist shaking. The car moved ahead. The woman snatched at her handbag. "*Attenzione*," she hissed.

He crossed with care to the dark side street and started down a deserted way. The noise had died off. He groped through an unfamiliar warren of unlit alleys shadowed by the blind walls of massive buildings. The narrow way opened into a piazza, leading to a tall and somber palace. Monumental blocks of roughened stone formed the base, at the top delicate columns framed a loggia; iron tethering rings were embedded in the sandstone walls. Where were the ladies of the lovely loggia, where the gallant cavaliers? Where was he? He had completely lost his bearings. What should he ask for if someone came along?

A clipped echoing sound of footsteps behind him. A man with a brief case hurried by, head bent, and passed without a glance. The old man held out his "*Dove?*" like a rag on a stick but the other never paused and soon vanished into a side street. An arterial clip-clop accompanied those rapidly disappearing footsteps, along with the familiar spongy weakness in the extremities. To steady himself he fumbled for one of the iron rings above his head. His misjudging fingers closed on nothing; he fell on the sharp paving stones. Pain throbbed in his kneecap. He lay spread-eagled where he fell. His body was spread out like the city with its intricate system of passageways and he astray in some narrow capillary far from the center.

But no, he was in a wood. How could he be in a city, and yet be in a wood? The wood was thick with trees; the trees were bent, mere bent gnarled sticks thrusting themselves, rigid and obstinate, from the ground. An ancient tree, more gnarled than the others, stood in the center of the clearing; from its cracked bark wept a thick brown gum. He wept too, he lay at its base and wept.

From close at hand he could hear the dull blows of an axe. The sounds knocked within him as though he were the hollow of a drum. Long intervals of silence; the woodsman must have leaned his axe against the tree he meant to fell and lain himself down to rest. With the cease of sound, a cease of air; suffocation filled the void. Then the rhythmic blows returned; the dead air moved anew.

He lay on his back, his head pressed against the tree. Faces hung like fruit in the branches. Something fluttered at the top among the dry thin twigs. At first it was only a movement, then it took on a vague outline of insect wings, the pupiled wings of a butterfly. The black pupils grew to eyes. His mother's eyes, or maybe Jean's. Punishing eyes. "Marder made me," he whimpered. "Don't you know how to say no?" Cold contemptuous voice. "How was I supposed to know?" "Can't you use your head?" The tedious argument dragged on. "Wait till your father hears." "You wait; wait till he knows." Knows what?" she screamed.

The woodman stood beside him and raised his axe. His arms and chest bulged. He towered among the branches that obscured his face.

"Wait," he implored.

The faces were weeping, he felt their hot tears

on his face. He sat up abruptly. The dog, who had just relieved himself, was trotting off around the corner of the building. His head had cleared. He knew now where he needed to go, the name of the bridge.

Again he heard footsteps approaching, more deliberate, a dull thud as though the person wore rubber soled shoes. A woman this time. She came to him when he beckoned

"Ponte Vecchio" he said. "*Dove*?"

She took him by the arm, led him to the bridge. She had a kind, matronly face. "*Pazienza*," she said, before she turned and went her way.

The bridge pulsed with life. Brightly lit shops lined the sides, throngs of people jostled to and fro. He had to pick his way with care. If he kept to the center he risked being rammed by young men pushing motorcycles; if he clung to the sides he would have to dodge the window-shoppers gaping at the lit showcases splendid with corals and pearls and the famous golden filigrees. Everywhere were girls: girls in shiny boots with round pink knees flickering out of long fur coats, girls draped in capes, their eyes shaded under wide brimmed borsalinos, girls insolent in tight white leather, with mascaraed eyes and hair spread across their shoulders,

He reached the center of the bridge. Here the shop-lined passageway widened, open to the river, and steps led to platforms on either side. People were leaning against the rails, some watching the river, some the passers-by. The young lounged on the steps. Indifference curtained their faces. He would never have dared to approach them anyway, with the question that in any case he did not know how to ask. Show me the way to go home . . .

The young American couple was still at their stand on the opposite platform. Several days ago they had appeared at evening and spread their wares and their workshop over a cloth on the steps. They were twisting strands of wire into long hoop earrings, elaborately spiraled necklaces, rings joined of many circles, which they sold for a few hundred lire. A scrawny, sallow pair, he in jeans and boots, she in a long skirt of dingy pattern, dank hair and a shawl.

A surly looking young man half sprawled on the steps below the spread-out cloth. His eyes automatically ticked off the passing girls; now and then he turned to watch the jewelry maker.

The old man too watched the girl. He got some comfort doing this, some calm, some balm, her fingers moving so quietly among the wires like fish among the reeds. Something in the bend of her head reminded him of Flossie. She looked up from her work. He thought she was looking at him. Her eyes were smudged, burnt out. Flossie had once looked at him like that. Thwarted, she had picked up a stone and thrown it at him. The stone bounced on the road, the look was like the stone. Unexpectedly the girl picked up one of the earrings, her lips parted in what might be a smile. She tilted her head to one side and waggled the trinket at him. The thin bare arm beckoned from without the shawl.

The fleshy young man sat watching her.

At that moment Arthur Brown decided he would buy his daughter the hoop earrings. The single hoop or the double hoops, it didn't matter. It meant he had to change his course. No simple thing. For was he not, finally, set on his way and heading presumably for home? To oppose, now, the stream of life in the direction it chose to go. Shouldn't he float along with the others, instead of stubbornly and feebly trying to push across their path like some waterfly dodging a tide of debris? For a long time he stood poised at the edge, watchful, fearful. Then he stepped in.

A party of Japanese tourists hung with cameras and carrying umbrellas engulfed him and swept him along. He clawed free, hauling himself through the welter of straps, and was finally ejected from the indignant group. He had lost his hat. It bobbed along on the tip of someone's furled umbrella. From the opposite direction four youths, arms enlaced, identical in black leather jackets, tight black pants, black shiny hair, bore down on him.. They advanced with measured steps. He scurried to get out of the way. The one on the end caught him with his swinging free arm and sent him reeling. They swaggered on.

He stood in a cleared space at the base of the steps. The faces around him were featureless as spectators at a Goya bullfight. Before him, half reclining on an elbow, blocking his way, sat the stolid young man, his attention now focused on our friend with a look so blank it was a question whether the retinal message ever reached the brain. Beyond him, cross-legged, impassive as an idol, the girl among her gewgaws. She had attached one of the earrings to her ear, the dull metal of the three hoops caught and released the light of the street lamp at her least movement. All else receded to the outskirts of consciousness. Before him only the florid face, the small eyes of the man blocking his path.

"I want to get by."

"What's stopping ya."

"You are. Please let me by."

The young man shifted his leg slightly. The old man started eagerly up the steps. The young man put out his leg again.

"Goin' somewhere, Pop?"

The girl laughed, a thin whinny.

"Let me by," he cried again. He tried to go around the outstretched leg but the young man moved to block him.

"Not so fast, Pop. What's on your mind?"

"I want to buy something. Flossie . . . ."

He tried to lunge over the leg that blocked his way.

The young man pulled up his knee; it caught him in the groin.

"Gw'an. Get lost."

He lay on the cold stone, quite stunned and still. Voices shrilled around him. If he could just find the word, he thought. The word approached, it seemed almost within his grasp, only to withdraw again. Flossie was in it somewhere.

Flossie. Yes, Yes, that was it; it was there, close by his dark little room, the small piazza and the church. The church. He was with Jean; inside, in the dim chapel, someone dropped a coin in a machine, and then the angel came out of the darkness, light of foot, winged, in gauzy raiment blown, shot with the radiance of a setting sun. The angel's head was turned away.

Yes, he thought, quite calm now, yes, yes, there it is, *felicità*, piazza Santa Felicità. He breathed it out so faintly no one looking down at him could hear. In his mind's eye, grown immense, the aloof angel on the wall, his swirling garments beneath the naked bulb a roseate splendor of salmon and gold. Then the light went out.

‡

Deceit of Snow

Deceit of Snow

Who is telling this story? It is my wicked-
tongued friend whose edges age has rather
sharpened than smoothed. She tells it in the lapidary
style necessary to contain, she says, romantic
excess. She was in her own person, elegant dress
and carriage, severe hairstyle, tiny pearl earrings,
admirably contained. In the village they called her
the Widow, as one might say the Baker or the
Stonecutter; she was widow by profession, three
husbands buried and, say some, a fourth, though
that was in another country. For that and her single
arm and that she dealt in dreams, certain village
gossips took her for a witch. I can picture her, tall
and stately, striding at the head of the funeral
processions, her black skirts flicking about her legs,
so beautiful that at first one was shocked and then
immediately forgot her handicap. I knew her as
Mme. Funaro, a person then in her sixties, still
beautiful, and wise, it seemed to me, in the ways of
the world.

In those days I would visit her regularly,
climbing the hill to her house in the heavy afternoon
heat. At the siesta hour no one was abroad, houses
slumbered behind dark shutters, bees droned in the
bushes. The garden gate was closed. No matter
how carefully I pulled the bolt it would crack like a
pistol shot, scattering the lizards off the hot rocks.
The gate swung wide on its creaking hinges, my feet

crunched the gravel path, my spirits would lift and tighten like a pennant in the wind. A high dense hedge on one side of the path guarded her privacy, on the other side flowers rioted, from the tangled branches of pear trees sang invisible birds. An Egyptian cat in green stone sat tall among the cosmos, relic of some rumored Alexandrine affair. Shadows slanted across a leaden sundial.

"Summer has ended," she said; she had come from the house to meet me. Generally she would be waiting at the tea table on the front veranda. "It snowed last night on the mountains." I looked back at the mountain range that rimmed this green valley. Snow covered the jagged peaks, its absolute white rendered the blue sky gaudy as a postcard.

"Snow on the mountains," she said, moments later, the tea poured. She struck me as unusually thoughtful. "It reminds me of a story I heard at a alpine inn many years ago. I was only in my twenties. I found it haunting. It happened to a young couple on their honeymoon at that same inn many years before. In the village the tale had become legend, and still on certain nights of early fall old wives that had been young wives would whisper and shake their heads. They too knew the long night's vigil. On my walks, walks that young pair must have taken, I would wonder, I wonder still: what could they have said to one another through the dark hours?"

Such were our afternoons, tea and perhaps a story from her hoard. I was the listener from another land, young, naive, yet not too naive to understand these stories, dense with the past, spiced with malice and laughter, her light delicious laughter, as paradigms in the education she was giving me. If they touched on the personal, it was trivially, or perhaps so disguised as to slip past my watchful curiosity. Most I have long since forgotten, except for one, this one returns, this riddling tale, across the oceans and the years, lit by the amber glow of those afternoons on the veranda where we sat looking through panes of glass into the green of the garden, the blue hydrangeas, the distant dark diamond-glittering lake.

Summer is brief in the high mountains, she began, its end can be precipitous. Fog and rain will close on the alpine meadows while the grain still ripens in the lowlands. Snow has been known to fall in the middle of August so that whoever ascends those regions at that season unprepared for risk and uncertainty is likely to descend again out of sorts and disgruntled.

The innkeeper at the spectacularly situated village of L— was surprised, therefore, to receive the telegram announcing the imminent arrival of the newlywed pair at the moment when everyone else was beginning to look askance at a still sparkling sky. And indeed that very day, as the little train crawled up the winding track cut narrowly into the steep hillside and those in the sunshine below looked up and said, "Storm's coming in the mountains," halfway up a fog closed down on them thick enough

to blot out the world. Since their marriage was only
of a day she found it quite magical and mysterious
now to be born aloft wrapped in a dense gray cloud.

"It's an incognito, a disguise," she cried. "Isn't
this the way the gods travel, wrapped in mist?"

So she chose to view the world, through mirrors
of legend and story. He loved this in her; himself he
thought hopelessly prosaic. As the other passengers
had been dropped off at stations along the way, with
their carpetbags and sacks of potatoes, he leaned
across and kissed her.

A trap met them at the station and whirled them
along the green cobbled streets and up the steep
drive where the inn with its famous view sat on a
knoll. The innkeeper who met them at the door
looked at her without recognition for he had married
into the old Inn family only recently and would have
no reason to remember the long-legged child with
the invalid aunt who came each year to stay in that
same front room the pair was now to occupy. In
later years his successors would regale newcomers
with the tale of that honeymoon, like a *specialité de
maison* that, far from hurting business, only added to
the inn's cachet.

By dinnertime all the guests knew about the
recent arrivals. The wedding had caused a stir,
ripples from which had ascended even to this
mountain retreat. He was the scion of a far-flung
clan with large commercial interests and immense
holdings in pastures and woodlands; she was a young
aristocrat, last of an ancient line, and, moreover,

interestingly orphaned at an early age. Some said her parents had drowned in a ferry crossing the Dardanelles; others, that they were buried in an avalanche while skiing on the Grossglockner. Doubly orphaned in fact, since the aunt who was raising her died too when she was still a child, and hadn't that happened, come to think of it, in this very inn?

They were the last to table and when they walked across the room, oblivious to stares, it was remarked how like brother and sister they looked, almost of a height, lean, clean and polished, shining of eyes and hair, with a pent and forward movement to the jaw. Whispers followed in their wake; some sat up a little straighter, others toyed with their wine glasses. On closer look her jaw appeared to have the more determined thrust; in his handsome face with the bright blue eyes, the smile that marked such winning creases in his cheeks, there was something, might one say, a little lax, about the chin.

Those that knew him, so went the whispers, and who could claim to know *her,* were hard put to understand the match, apart, of course, from the obvious considerations, for, despite their striking and even disconcerting physical resemblance, there seemed little common ground between them. Unlike the statesmen and industrialists among his kin, he had reverted to the original type, a son of the land, a farmer at heart, of plain tastes, few words, and when excited, a quite inhibiting stutter. She walked wrapped in the legend of her aloofness, her ancient name, a reputation for recklessness, and an austere and elegant beauty. Had the airplane been invented she would have been among the first to fly. Who would have credited him with the imagination to woo her? Or dreamed she would consent? He had a stubbornness to equal hers; besides, he was enthralled.

In the week that followed the sun failed to reappear; the lowering skies remained a uniform melancholy gray interrupted by periods of a fine chill rain. Those guests whose term was not yet up began to suffer from irritability and malaise, went for walks and returned soon after, damp and dispirited, looked at the sky a hundred times a day, were too restless for card games by the fire, and began to find the food monotonous.

The young couple on the other hand was enchanted. They leaned across the railing of their balcony, over the baskets of red geraniums, and peered through the soft fog into a perfect invisibility; they drew back into their room warm with pine, lamplight and red-patterned cloth, and pulled the fog about them as if it were a cocoon. After the first evening they no longer appeared in the dining room; in fact they were seldom seen. Trays, now full, now empty, appeared with regularity on the floor outside their door; their appetites were hearty. After lunch, when everyone had retired for the siesta, they would quietly emerge to vanish again into the dripping woods; at dusk they would return with wet bright cheeks and arms laden with cones and branches.

Dinner they took at a small table in front of the fireplace, while the few remaining guests toyed with their food in the cold dining room, too demoralized to muster the necessary energy to pack up and leave.

Bad weather in the mountains has been known to settle in for weeks. Gradually the inn and the village emptied of visitors; the last stragglers boarded the small train that puffed them off the mountain, relieved to escape at last the blank hostility of those skies. The other inns of the village closed. Since he saw these two would remain, the innkeeper cut his staff and waited on them himself; there was no need to give up good paying guests.

If others noticed them, *they* noticed nobody. The villagers remarked their goings out and their comings in, hooded alike against the drizzle and scarcely to be told one from the other. The woman who kept the mercer's shop came to recognize the slight syncopation of their steps on the pavement; when they passed before her window one sharp profile slightly preceded the other like two heads superimposed on a coin. For she was always a trifle ahead, tugging as it were with a taut impatience against some invisible leash while he, in spite of his compact athletic body, his assured movements, seemed, in company with her, to lag. At evenfall, the trap might take them, snugly wrapped in a coverlet, through alleys soundless but for the delicious melancholy dripping of the trees, the muffled roll of wheels through sodden woods.

On one of their walks they followed a stream that rushed through the forest into a meadow. Near a wooden bridge he had picked up a triangular green stone, the same stone that paved the village streets, and now it stood propped against their mantel.

"It's the shape of the mountain," she said." It's out there facing us, but who would know? That immense mountain wiped out by fog. The fog, it's nothing, you can put your hand through it, but it's stronger than the mountain."

"The fog will fade," he said. "In the end the mountain always wins."

She was sitting by the hearth and as she bent forward to stare into the coals her silken hair, the color of wet sand, fell across her cheek. Her stillness was as intense as her moving. Light struck the nape of her neck, its pure exquisite curve. What could be more ravishing, he thought, or more vulnerable. Watching her he held his breath. This creature, so frighteningly unencumbered, stood out among all he knew, all that was solid and grounded in earth and time, in tribe and land, with the merciless clarity of an arrow in flight.

Her eyes rested on him now with a mildness he had never seen in her. It was as though some wild thing had come to rest; as though, he thought, almost with a shudder, he wore her on his wrist. For her part she had never felt so safe, nor had she ever known she wanted to.

In the closeness of that week she began to talk

as she never had before. It was only now he learned
of the summers she had spent here as a child with
the frail aunt she adored. She told him of solitary
rambles in the woods gathering the stones and
leaves and flowers that she would pour at day's end
into her aunt's lap. Together they would parse each
one, its name and qualities. At night by the fire her
aunt would read to her, tales of magic and faery, of
heroes, quests: these shaped her dreams.

At the last she told him of the black pool. With
an English family she had climbed above the
timberline to a rock-strewn plateau at the edge of a
glacier. The three-faced mountain loomed above
them; blinded by the sun on its glittering slope they
hid their eyes. "It's as big as God," cried the
smallest child. From here went only those who had
rope and ax and could crawl like flies up vertical
steeps and stand the sight of vertiginous drops.

On that windy plateau they came upon a pool, a
small hollow in the granite, filled with glacial melt,
black and smooth as marble. Reflected in the still
water the snowy peak gave the illusion of almost
limitless depth. One of the children shook a few
drops from his canteen into the water. Terror seized
her; the waters would rise to overwhelm them, they
would turn to stone. Her ears began to ring and her
face turned white.

"Altitude sickness," they said and rubbed her
hands and face and made her sit down. When they
reached the inn late in the afternoon everything was
in confusion. Her aunt, who had been sitting quietly

in the garden, had as quietly died.

"They took me away that night. I've never been back. We must go there. We must find the black pool."

Seeing my puzzled look my friend stopped, "A child of excited imagination," she murmured, "over given to reading. You may know the story. It's the classic formula: the two wicked older brothers possessed by greed; the task in quest of promised fortune, in this case to empty three drops of holy water into the Golden River at the mountaintop. Each toils up the mountain wracked by thirst, carrying a flask of water unlawfully gotten; each refuses even a drop to the sick dog, the dying child, met along the way. When, finally, they empty their flasks into the river, the waters rise and cover them; they are turned into two black stones. Why should a child fear such a fate?"

She fell silent. And then, "The night hags that pursue us in our youth, they may outlive our childhood."

Again a silence, so long it became uncomfortable. Her thoughts had wandered. I was loath to interrupt. But when she took up her tale her voice had renewed vigor, like the runner who sees with but a few more laps the end in sight.

In the small of the night of the seventh day winds from a different quarter swept the sky. They woke to see the last gold-shot nacreous shreds of mist dissolve into a purity of blue. From their balcony the famous peak glittered icily above the trees. In a fever of haste now they would go, now if ever, for in two days they were to leave. Bread and cheese and fruit were brought, knapsacks packed, boots laced. "We might go on to T—, in which case we'll spend the night there," she told the landlord, and they discussed the paths that led to the next hamlet.

The journey that day was like no other. Morning and mountain had burst with radiant suddenness from the confines of fog and so it seemed had they. They sped with long tireless strides up the mountainside, and the sun climbed with them. The forest floor exhaled a fresh smell of loam; dew spangled the spider webs; the waxy pine needles gleamed. She led the way as though it were yesterday and not a dozen years since a child had passed this way. So swift and silent was their passage over the sodden leaves they seemed to leave no imprint.

But there may have been an encounter. An old woman who had been gathering sticks on the mountain burst that morning into the village ranting about a meeting in the forest. People usually paid scant attention to her raving but it was clear something had badly frightened her. A rumor spread that she had seen the Huntsman riding through the woodland. But I think, my friend said, that she crossed the path of that bright and beautiful pair. Don't they say the old and foolish have a second sight? A week later she fell and broke her hip and ten days after she was dead.

The dense cover of larch and pine began to thin; the trees grew stunted and soon fell away; they had reached the timberline. They paused on a knoll of close-cropped grass; wideness spread about them like a bowl of light.

She stood on a rock ledge that hung out upon the air like a shelf. The wind had risen, it whipped back her hair and clothes, sculpting her against the emptiness. Birds circled the treetops small as gnats; on the valley floor a stream was a thin silver seam. She beckoned but he shook his head. The narrow ledge held no room for him. She turned to look at him; he saw her fierce, exultant face.

Now they walked the zone of unliving rock where no path could be worn. Tufts of pink androsace grew in the crevices; lichen stained the granite yellow. At the crest of the ridge a climber's hut made a small blot against the backdrop of the mountain. "There," she said, " up there beyond that rise," and hurried on.

He followed more slowly, uneasy now at what might be ahead. When he reached the top she had vanished, but then he saw her in the shadow of an enormous boulder, scanning the desolate debris of rocks, gravel, scree left by the mountains' crumbling, the glacier's continual scourings. Of black pool there was none.

Common sense would have predicted it, but common sense was for dolts. He had said the wrong thing, and he reddened under her stare.

She moved away from him, still searching the

ground, kicking at stones. He lagged behind, annoyed with himself, distressed at her petulance, saw her drop to her knees, beckon wildly, then she was gone. He found her kneeling inside a small cave. Masses of white blossoms tumbled about her head and shoulders, immense tufts of crowfoot that grew from every fissure of roof and wall.

A spring, clear as glass, welled from the center of the cave. The wreath he wove for her head was found later on the ice. They knelt together and with cupped hands gave each other drink. The water was pure and fresh as morning.

When they were ready to leave, unthinking, he shook the last drops from his flask to fill it from the spring. He heard her gasp, then laugh, her wild clear laugh. She dipped her hand into the spring and flung the drops in his face. "The mountain now anoints you," she cried.

They stood at the edge of the glacier. Clouds now obscured the valley but at this height all was sun and clarity, immensity and glitter. It was as though in climbing they had stepped over a threshold onto a different brilliance of world. Snow had fallen on the ice field; its broad expanse undulated toward the mountain, lapping against its base like a mild sea of gentle billows, white and softly gleaming.

So they went out on the ice, my friend went on, sipping her tea. It was too tempting. Still, if it's flat, it's safe enough. On the slopes the way becomes perilous; spring avalanches bring down huge piles of snow and rock, crevices open up, there are precipices, abysses hidden beneath the snow.

At the glacier's edge she wedged her stick between two rocks and tied her red scarf to it. She may have courted danger but she wasn't completely reckless. His cap hung from the top where he flung it, rakishly, in sun that can be as pitiless as the desert's. What did he know of such things, this son of the lowland?

It must have been an exultancy, the empty whiteness, the deep blue vault of the sky, the silence that only their laughter shattered. They were mere specks upon the snow, gnats on a tablecloth. Perhaps the very vastness made them heedless, as though their insignificance would keep them from harm. They played like giddy children, chasing each other with shouts across the ice field, foolish as the butterfly that sometimes strays across the glacier, far from the meadow where it had browsed. On it flies, ever forward, and finding no place to settle, exhausted, falls to the ice to die.

Clarity is deceptive at those heights. In that extreme whiteness perspective is lacking, there is nothing to measure against. The very purity of the air makes for error, the far seems near, and so the mountain, miles away, can appear quite close and close to it they saw a strange circular patch of green spangled with colors.

The slope was gradual, without realizing they had begun to climb. They began to pass turrets of ice flashing emerald green and walk alongside crevices masked only by a thin and tender snow.

Lured by that many-colored patch that seemed so close, they hurried on.

It was no mirage, this island of flowers in the snow. The mountain people call it the Courtil, a garth, though few have actually seen it. A circular plateau of granite carpeted with turf lies slightly raised above the ice; a stone and gravel wall encloses it. The plants grow low, with fleshy, leathery leaves and woody stems against the harshest cold; they wait the moment when snow melt and sun warmth will call forth flowers, hastily, briefly, blue forget-me-nots, pink moss campions, purple saxifrage, the white alpine rose, powdered with gold from the thicket of stamens at its core and the yellow buttercup whose heat, they say, can melt the snow. Magical in that place, magical as the paddocked garden of the unicorn.

And guarded too by a moat; a deep crevice circles it. They prowled around, seeking some point of access; where a narrow ice bridge spanned the chasm their frozen footprints stop. How all this must have fed her fancy, the pure spring, the green ice turrets, the flowery island behind its moat, the narrow bridge across the chasm, the golden flower. They had no ropes, pitons, grappling hooks. One would stay to anchor the other; one would go. There would have been no question now, for him or for her, who. He would pluck the flower that lay beside her.

Perhaps, even with his farmer's sense, his sportsman's caution, he stepped gaily, sure-footed as an aerialist, across the bridge. He had her at his back then, the garden just ahead. But coming back, heady with success, he would see her slight figure dark against the waste; below him, if he dared to look, the abyss. He would come slowly, testing each step with his stick. When he was close, she would hold out her hand, her light capricious hand. He would place in it the prize.

He stepped off the bridge; the snow at the edge, continually and imperceptibly melting, gave way beneath his feet. He flung himself forward; his grasping hands gathered the loose snow as he slid. She caught at him and leaned back to brace him. His weight dragged her to the brink. Four feet down a narrow ledge broke his fall.

It was the sixteenth hour. She lay prone on the ice clutching his hand. The slippery wall offered neither ledge nor crack by which to climb. She would have needed the strength of two men to pull him up.

She lay there, staring into the sinking sun. She would call for help, again and again, the young strong voice fading into the nothingness until he would beg her to stop. Did she assure him then that they would be missed, that people would come to look for them; did he remind her that she had countered any such possibility? The sun blazed out behind the mountain, the snowy summit turned rose, shadows darkened the crevice, moved across the snow, darkness covered them. Then did he see again how she combed her shining fall of hair by the fire, the look in her luminous eyes? What could they have said, one to the other, through the long hours before her grip slackened and he fell?

There were voices that night in the mountains mingled with the distant thunder of crashing rocks. A chamois hunter caught by nightfall far from home had taken shelter against a rock. During the night he heard in the creaks and shiftings of the glacier sounds like cries and weeping, then a braided murmur like the voices, as he put it, of the waterfall that soothed him into drowsiness. He woke to hear a woman singing and he was much afraid.

At dawn he tracked the frozen footsteps in the snow. He found her spread-eagled on the ground and carried her down the mountain, one stiff arm outstretched, the arm she had held him by.

"You lay it at her door," I said, half in question. I was careful not to look at the empty sleeve.

"Some doors one opens at one's peril." Her grave voice was tinged with mockery.

"Then was she . . . ?"

"Who could survive such a night?"

Silence spread around us. Her white face looked stern in the dusk. The bells of evening tolled from the lakeside. She got up; the story had ended.

‡

About The Author

Barbara Kremen grew up in New Jersey, was educated at Bryn Mawr College and Harvard University and other institutions of higher or lesser learning, worked as a journalist, a teacher, and in museum research, lived variously in France, Switzerland and Italy, and makes her home in North Carolina with her artist husband. She has published *Out Of*, a book of poems, *Tree Trove,* a botanical fiction for adults and children, and poetry and literary criticism in *The Sewanee Review, Pembroke Magazine, Romance Notes, The Philological Quarterly, The New York Times,* and *The Saint Andrews Review.*

About the Artist

Collagist, painter and sculptor, Irwin Kremen began making art at the age of forty-one while a professor of psychology at Duke University. He is entirely self-trained. The first exhibitions of his work were organized by the National Collection of Fine Arts of the Smithsonian Institution in Washington; close to thirty solo venues have followed at museums and contemporary art centers, nationally and abroad. Among the museums that hold his work in their collections are the San Francisco Museum of Fine Arts, the Philadelphia Museum, the Smithsonian American Art Museum, the Houston Museum of Fine Arts, and the Carnegie Museum of Art.